The Restless Robin

By MARJORIE FLACK

HOUGHTON MIFFLIN COMPANY

The Riverside Press Cambridge

Sixteenth Printing w

One February day in the State of Georgia, where Spring had come and the peach trees were in bloom, a certain Mr. Cock Robin said, 'Cheerio,' and then he lifted his wings and set out for the North. Mr. Robin set out alone to find a place for a home.

He flew over the State of South Carolina and the State of North Carolina and over the City of Washington in the District of Columbia.

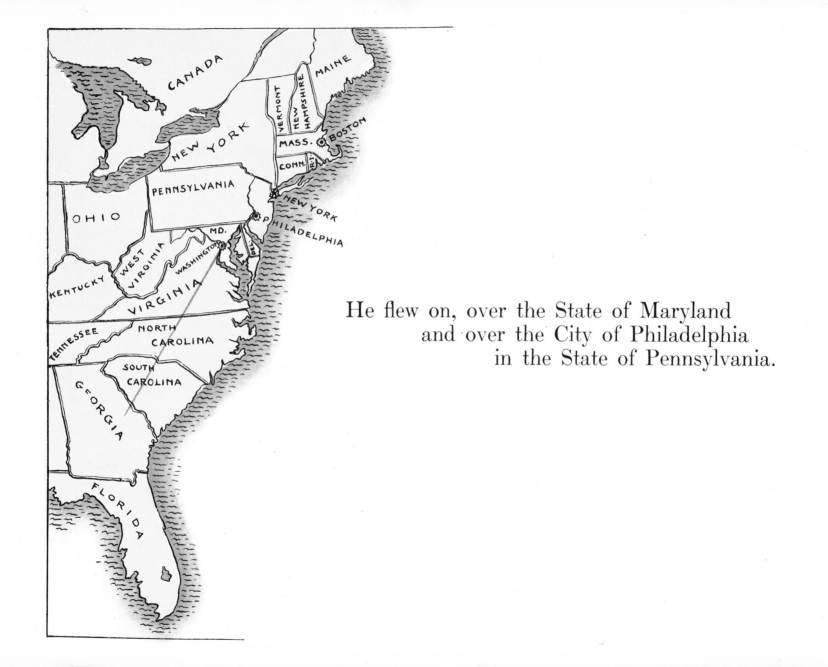

He flew on, over the State of Maryland
and over the City of Philadelphia
in the State of Pennsylvania.

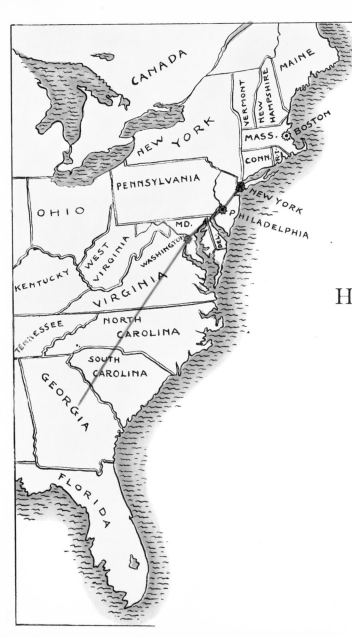

He flew on, over the State of New Jersey
and over the City of New York
in the State of New York.

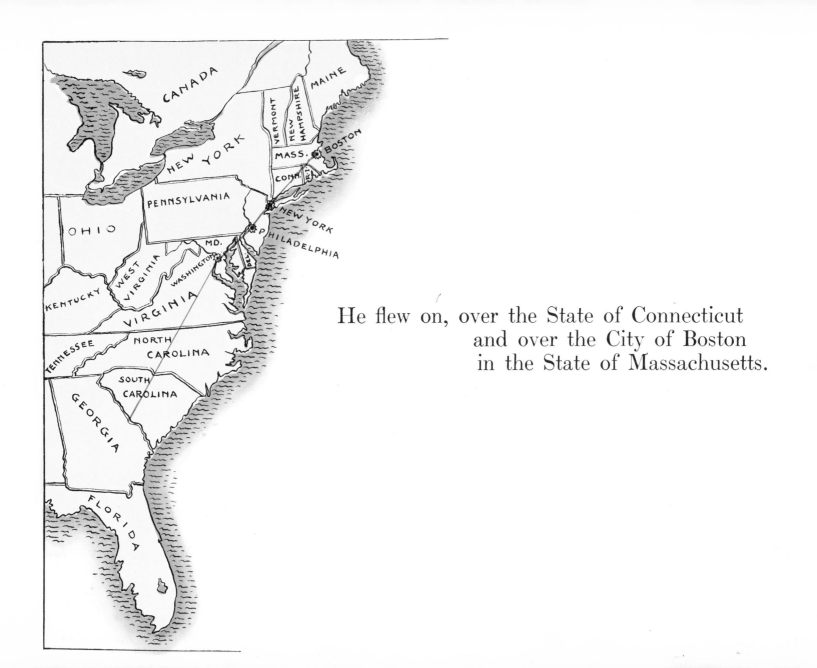

He flew on, over the State of Connecticut
and over the City of Boston
in the State of Massachusetts.

He flew on until he came to the mountains in the State of New Hampshire, and there he stopped. Mr. Cock Robin stopped his flight to the North and he looked about him to find a fitting place to be his home.

Although it was the twentieth of March, no trees were in bloom and the Winter's snow was on the mountains and the wind blew cold, for Spring had not yet come in the State of New Hampshire.

Nevertheless Mr. Cock Robin sang his Spring song: 'Cheerily, cheerily — Cheer up!' and he went about his business of finding a fitting place to be his home.

He considered
the Hemlock trees

and the Pine trees
on the mountain.

He considered the
slim Birch trees near
the lake.

He considered the Oak trees
and the Elm trees of the village,

but he found not one of these trees to his liking.

At last he found an Orchard, an Orchard of Apple trees near a Farmhouse in the valley, and Mr. Cock Robin sang loud and long because he found this place to his liking.

'Cheerily — cheerily — cheerily — cheer up — cheerily!' he sang, telling the world that this Orchard belonged to him; that this Orchard was now his property. From daybreak to nightfall, Mr. Robin sang; and he protected his property from all trespassers

until Mrs. Robin came back to him from the South.

Mrs. Robin was pleased with this Orchard because it was near their last year's home, she was pleased with Mr. Robin, and he was pleased that she had found him, and he sang loud and long because they were happy to be together again.

Then Mrs. Robin chose the Apple tree nearest the Farmhouse as best of all the trees in the Orchard in which to build their home.

There on a branch of this Apple tree they began to build their nest. They gathered bits of string and dried grasses and Mrs. Robin carried mud in her bill and plastered them all together. She plastered the inside carefully and rounded the walls with her breast until she had a beautiful smooth round mud cup of a house and then they lined it with clean soft grass — and it was finished. Then Mr. Robin sang because he was proud of their nest in the Apple tree near the Farmhouse in the valley of the mountains in the State of New Hampshire.

Then one day Mrs. Robin laid a beautiful blue egg in the nest, and the next day she laid another and the next day she laid another, so at the end of three days she had three beautiful blue eggs in the nest. And Mr. Robin sang because he was proud of their nest and proud of their eggs.

Then Mrs. Robin kept
these three eggs warm
for thirteen
sunny days

and rainy days
and thirteen
nights.

April days turned into May days, the buds on the bare branches of the Apple tree began to swell with coming blossoms. The earth in the valley grew soft and damp from the melting snow on the mountains and early Spring flowers pushed up to the sun. And on the thirteenth day three baby Robins pecked their way out of the blue eggs in the nest in the Apple tree near the Farmhouse.

Three baby Robins opened their wide mouths and gaped in the strange air about them, and Mr. Robin sang because he was proud of his babies and proud of his nest and proud of himself.

But after that Mr. Robin had little time for singing. He was far too busy protecting his family and helping Mrs. Robin carry worms and grubs and bugs to feed three hungry mouths.

At first these three Robin babies had no real feathers whatsoever. Their eyes were tight shut and their funny little heads wobbled on their long skinny necks, but they knew enough

to open their big mouths and cry for food.

On the fifth day they opened their bright eyes, but all they used them for was to watch for more food to come.

Soon each little Robin began to sprout real little feathers, but not one of them noticed because all they could think of was more food and more food.

By the time they were ten days old, these three Robin babies had grown plump and better looking, but they were as greedy as ever.

Now that their children were older and stronger, Mr. and Mrs. Robin tried to teach them to be quiet and well behaved as young Robins should be.

They taught them not to grab for each other's food and not to cry without reason and to lie quietly in the nest while their father and mother were away.

Two of their three Robin children were girls, and their names were Muffy and Puffy. The third was a boy, and his name was Buffy. Muffy and Puffy soon learned to be well behaved as young Robins should be, but Buffy was a noisy and restless young fellow.

When Mr. and Mrs. Robin were away looking for worms, Muffy and Puffy, without a peep out of them, would settle quietly down in the nest to rest, but Buffy did not like to rest. He would wriggle about and he would stretch his head over the edge and he would open his mouth and keep up a constant peeping for no reason at all.

One day he made such a noise that the Farmhouse cat heard him and

came climbing up the tree closer
and closer to the nest —
but along came Mr. Robin

just in time.

'Tut-tut-tut-tut-tut!'

he scolded and chased the cat away.

One day a great storm came; thunder rumbled over the mountains and rain came pouring down. Mrs. Robin sheltered her children. She sheltered them with her outspread wings, but Buffy the restless young Robin wriggled his head out and got it wet. 'Tut-tut,' said Mrs. Robin and scolded him severely.

Then one warm day late in May the buds on the Apple tree burst into gay and fragrant blossoms and Muffy and Puffy and Buffy were now so large and plump and covered with so many feathers that they were much too crowded and much too warm in their nest in the Apple tree. They were so crowded that Buffy was even more restless than before.

While Mrs. Robin was looking for worms in the field and Mr. Robin was taking a bath in the watering-trough, Buffy, that restless Robin, hopped right up out of the nest and onto the edge of it. He stretched himself and he fluttered his little wings and he teetered back and forth on his long thin legs. He looked down at the Tulip bed below him and up at the Apple blossoms above him, and then he looked into the window of the Farmhouse.

There in the window he saw two faces, a boy's face and a girl's face; he saw four eyes looking at him; he saw two noses pressed against the pane and he saw two mouths laughing at him. Buffy was

so surprised that he slipped. He slipped off the edge of the nest and he fluttered down — down toward the ground. Buffy tried to make his wings fly, but he could not fly, so he landed lightly first on top of a Tulip and then he slid to the earth.

'Peep — peep, peep, peep, peep!' cried Buffy. 'Peep — peep!'

But Mrs. Robin in the field and Mr. Robin in the watering-trough had heard him cry so often without reason that they paid no attention to him whatsoever. But the cat heard Buffy cry and she came creeping, creeping up through the grass.

'Peep, peep, peep!' cried Buffy.

Then the children came running out from the Farmhouse and just as the cat was ready to spring, the boy caught him and the little girl picked up Buffy. She lifted Buffy up very carefully in her two hands.

'Peep — peep — peep!' cried Buffy, and he wriggled and tried to flutter his wings. 'Peep — peep — peep!'

'Oh, what shall I do, what shall I do with him?' asked the little girl. 'He wiggles!'

'I will take Kitty into the house!' said the boy, 'and then you had better put the little bird in the Lilac bush, perhaps his mother will come and get him.'

So the boy took the cat into the house and the little girl carefully placed Buffy in the Lilac bush — on the highest branch which she could reach and then she too went into the house.

'Peep — peep — peep, peep, O — peep, peep,' cried Buffy.

His mother came flying back to the nest.

'Peep, peep — peep, peep — peep, peeep!' cried Buffy.

'Wait — wait — wait — wait — wait — wait!' answered his mother. Then she fed Muffy and Puffy the worm she had brought to them.

But before she had finished, Mr. Robin came flying to the Lilac bush. He came to the aid of his little son. He perched near him and he fluttered his wings and then he sang to him.

He sang:

Cheerily, cheerily, cheerily, cheer up! Cheerily

cheerily, cheerily, cheerily, cheer up, cheerily!

'Peep, peep — peep, peep!' cried Buffy. 'Peep, peep!' and he tried to fly; and he could not fly. 'Peep, peep — peep, peep!' cried Buffy louder and louder than ever.

Then an Oriole heard Buffy and came to help him. The Oriole perched on the Lilac bush and he sang for Buffy his sailor's song:

2 octaves above

Heave ho! Heave ho!

Once more, once more, once more, now!

A Chickadee came to see what the trouble was, and he perched near the Oriole and joined in with his chatter. He said to Buffy:

8 va

Chick-a-de-de-de-de

A Thrasher, hearing all the noise,
came to help Buffy too. He perched
overhead and he sang his farmer's song:

2 octaves above

Hurry up, Hurry up, plough it, plough it, harrow it, harrow it, hoe it, hoe it, hoe it.

A
Peabody bird
joined
the Thrasher
and sang
for Buffy:

2 octaves above

Old Sam Peabody, Peabody, Peabody.

A Black-throated Green Warbler
came and he too joined in with his
slower song:

2 octaves above

Trees, trees, murmering trees.

A Bluebird came to see if he could help and he perched on a branch of the Apple tree and gently sang for Buffy his tender song:

2 octaves above

Tru - al - ly - Tru - al - ly -

Then a Song Sparrow flew near Buffy singing the sweetest of all the songs he knew:

Sweet, sweet, sweet, very merry cheer to you, you, you.

A Flicker, hearing Buffy's cries and all the birds singing so loudly, perched on a limb of the Apple tree and he gaily shouted at Buffy:

Quit - quit - quit - quit - quit - quit - quit - quit

quit - quit - quit - quit - quit - quit - quit - quit.

A Meadowlark, hearing such a great commotion, came from the field and perched beside the noisy Flicker and whistled to Buffy his Spring song:

Spring o' the ye-ar, Spring o' the y-e-a-r!

Then the Oriole and the Chickadee and the Thrasher and the Peabody bird and the Black-throated Green Warbler and the Bluebird and the Song Sparrow sang their songs over and over again for Buffy while the Flicker rattled along and the Meadowlark's sweet whistle rose and fell and rose and fell again and again as he sang: 'Spring o' the Ye-ar, Spring o' the Y-e-a-r!'

Buffy's father and mother flew over their little son. Back and forth they flew, flying to the music of the songs of the birds.

Buffy no longer cried. He listened to the birds as they sang their songs for him. Louder and louder grew the music, beating the air about him; filling the air of the valley and echoing from the mountains.

Buffy lifted his little wings and he fluttered them to the rhythm of the songs of the birds. Up and down he beat them to the throbbing, beating music. Faster, faster, beat the music, faster, faster, faster, faster and then Buffy

rose, he rose up
    into the air
      and he flew.

Following his father, followed by his mother,
Buffy flew to the music of the birds: he flew
up to the Apple tree, back home again.

As Buffy settled safely on a branch near his nest, the music hushed and the Oriole and the Chickadee and the Thrasher and the Peabody bird and the Black-throated Green Warbler and the Bluebird and the Song Sparrow and the Flicker and the Meadowlark flew happily away.

For two more days Buffy lived on the branch near the nest and he was as quiet and well behaved as a young Robin should be.

Then on the third day Muffy hopped up on the edge of the nest, fluttered her little wings and flew; then Puffy flapped her wings and followed after and then Buffy gaily spread his wings and flew through the air with his sisters.

And Mr. Robin sang because he was proud
of his strong big children as they flew
from the nest in the Apple tree
near the Farmhouse in the valley
of the mountains, in the State
of New Hampshire.

AUTHOR'S NOTE

I wish to express my thanks to Dr. Robert Cushman Murphy and to Dr. John T. Zimmer of the American Museum of Natural History, for their kindness in helping me make the story and pictures in this little book as nearly correct as possible.

I am deeply indebted to F. Schuyler Mathews for permission to use his notations of bird music from his book entitled *Fieldbook of Wild Birds and Their Music*, published by G. P. Putnam's Sons.

And I am also grateful to a certain pair of Robins who chose to build their nest in the tree outside my window.

Marjorie Flack